D1243952

Ely, IA 52227

HARALD HARDNUT

TONY BRADMAN

With illustrations by
Martin Remphry

Barrington Stoke

For my favourite band of Vikings –
Thomas, Oscar, Mark and Hayden!

First published in 2008 in Great Britain by
Barrington Stoke Ltd
18 Walker Street, Edinburgh, EH3 7LP

www.barringtonstoke.co.uk

This edition first published 2014
Reprinted 2016

Text © 2008 Tony Bradman
Illustrations © 2008 Martin Remphry

The moral right of Tony Bradman and Martin Remphry to
be identified as the author and illustrator of this work has
been asserted in accordance with the Copyright, Designs
and Patents Act, 1988

All rights reserved. No part of this publication may be
reproduced in whole or in any part in any form without
the written permission of the publisher

A CIP catalogue record for this book is available
from the British Library upon request

ISBN: 978-1-78112-416-1

Printed in China by Leo
1046696

Contents

6.1.8.19

Chapter 1
The Raven of Death

The north of England – September 1066

It was late in the evening when the messenger rode into York. His horse's hoof-beats rang out, loud and echoey, down the narrow streets. He pulled his horse to a stop by a big hall, jumped from the saddle and ran inside. There was a feast going on in the hall – lots of people were eating and drinking and laughing loudly.

The messenger didn't wait for anyone to ask him what he wanted. He walked right up to the top table. "My lord, I bring evil news," he said to a richly dressed man who was sitting there, a cup of wine in his hand. The man's name was Morcar, and he was the Earl of Northumbria, the most powerful Saxon chief in the north of England.

The messenger went on, "A Viking army has landed ... and it's on its way here!"

"What?" said Morcar as he leapt to his feet. There were gasps and grim faces all around the hall. The Vikings were tough warriors, raiders and invaders who had been bringing fire and death to England for over 250 years.

"Call out the men!" yelled Morcar. "There's no time to lose!"

It was 1066, a strange and dangerous year for England. King Edward had died in January, and the great Saxon warlord Harold Godwinson had made himself the new king. But there were others who thought they should be king. Duke William of Normandy had been King Edward's cousin. He thought he should be King of England now. After all, King Edward had promised him he would be.

Everyone expected William and his army to invade in the south. So who was leading this army in the north?

****

"We'll try and hold them here," Morcar said to his second in command, his brother Edwin. It was dawn and Morcar's army was taking up its position in front of them, across the road to York. Their spies said the Viking army was very close.

"I've sent a messenger to London for help," said Morcar.

"King Harold would come if he could," said Edwin. Morcar and Edwin were friends of the new king. "But I don't think he can. He's too far away, and he needs all his men in the south for when Duke William invades. It looks like we're on our own, brother ..."

"There they are!" Edwin pointed at a hill in the distance. The Viking army was running down it towards them, crowds of fierce warriors yelling and screaming for blood. Sunlight glittered on their helmets and swords and axes and spears. One Viking carried a tall pole with a flag fluttering at the top.

The flag was huge and red. On it was a terrifying picture – the raven of death.

Morcar stared at the flag. "Oh no, it can't be!" he murmured. "He's too old, isn't he?"

"I know whose flag that is, too," Edwin said grimly. "It must be him. We're for it now. Quick, men, form the shield wall!" Edwin yelled.

There was the clunk of wood kissing wood as the Saxons joined their shields together. Soon Morcar and Edwin could see the Viking chief at the front of the attack. A giant of a man with long golden hair flowing from under his helmet. There was a huge grin on his face and a sword in his hand.

Morcar and Edwin gulped. They knew now who it had to be. They had no chance. Heading towards them was Harald Hardrada – the greatest Viking of them all.

Chapter 2
Born to Be a Warrior

Who was Harald Hardrada? Why was he the greatest Viking of them all?

Harald was born in Norway, in 1015, and was the son of an important and noble family. His older half-brother Olaf was the King of Norway. Just as in England, there was a constant, deadly fight for power among the country's great warlords.

Harald grew up to be a fierce warrior –
and the Vikings gave him a nickname. They
called him *Hardrada*. That means 'hard nut'
in Old Norse, the Vikings' language. But even
when Harald was very small his family knew
that he was going to be a hardnut – tough and
dangerous.

The story goes that when Harald was still a
boy, his half-brother King Olaf of Norway came
to visit. Olaf was a grown man and a fierce
warrior who had fought in many battles. He
decided to have some fun with his half-brother,
and made horrible, scary faces at him.

But Harald wasn't bothered. He just stared
right back at King Olaf.

"Well, it seems that I can't frighten you,
little brother," said Olaf, with a laugh. "Tell me,
what would you like to be when you grow up?"

"A warrior, like you," said Harald – and Olaf
could see he meant it.

Harald got the training he needed. By the time he was a teenager, he knew all about war. He wore a chainmail shirt and an iron helmet, and carried a shield. He learned how to use a Viking warrior's weapons – sword and spear and battle-axe. He grew to be very tall and strong, a giant when he was still young.

Harald's skills and size came in useful, too. There was plenty of danger in Norway at that time. Some of the great warlords plotted to kill King Olaf, and the king had to flee the country. But he quickly returned with an army to try and take back his kingdom. Harald joined him.

Olaf's army met the rebel warlords in a valley. Olaf gave the order to charge, and his men crashed into the warlords' shield wall. Swords clanged and men shouted and screamed. Olaf's warriors fought bravely but they were out-numbered. Soon everyone could see that Olaf had lost the battle.

Harald saw Olaf fall under a cloud of arrows. He was hurt as well. Even so, he was desperate to fight on. He knew the odds were against him but he did not want to give up. One of Olaf's warriors dragged him away.

"Quickly, my Lord Harald," said the man. "There's nothing but death here."

Harald stopped to look at the battle-field which was covered with blood-stained corpses. The rebel warriors stood over them. They banged their swords on their shields and roared out a wild song of victory. Ravens flew round and round in the sky above, waiting for their chance to land and feast on the bodies.

"You're right," Harald muttered grimly. "We have lost here. But this is not the end. I'll be back. I might be a nobody now, but I swear one day those warlords will know who I am!"

So Harald had to leave Norway. He was 15 years old. The year was 1030.

Chapter 3
More Battles ... and a Princess

Kiev, Russia – 1033

"Well, what do you think then, lads?" said Harald with a grin at his two best friends, Ulf and Haldor. All three were wearing helmets and chainmail. They carried swords and shields. Harald was 18 years old now, a tall man and a brave fighter. He laughed. "Shall we just stand here and let those raiders come at us," he said. "Or shall we show them what we Vikings are made of?"

In front of them was a group of raiders on the look-out for another village to loot and burn. Harald and his friends were working for the Prince of Kiev. It was their job to protect this village. They'd seen the raiders draw closer and closer and now the three young Vikings had to chase them back – or die.

"I don't know ..." said Ulf. "There's a lot more of them than us."

"Ulf's right," muttered Haldor. "And isn't it time for dinner, too?"

"What a pair of chickens!" laughed Harald. "I'll fight them on my own, then. That's fine – all the more fun for me!"

With that, Harald gave a terrible war cry and charged the raiders. He held his sword high in the air and yelled as he ran at them. Ulf and Haldor looked at each other. They gave

a sigh. Then they both grinned and charged off
behind Harald, waving their swords and yelling
war cries too.

The raiders never stood a chance.

Harald, Ulf and Haldor had come to Kiev from Sweden. That's where they'd met and made friends with one another. The three of them had stuck together. They went south, into the enormous land of Russia. And at last they'd come to the city of Kiev, where Prince Yaroslav was the ruler.

The prince had always been King Olaf's friend, so he offered Harald a place to live. Harald joined his army, and Ulf and Haldor did the same. For the next couple of years they'd fought many battles for the prince, and defeated all of his enemies.

At last Harald decided it was time to ask the prince to reward him for everything he'd done.

And Harald knew just what reward he wanted. He'd fallen in love with the prince's beautiful daughter Elizabeth. She liked Harald, too.

"You want to marry my daughter?" growled the prince. He scowled at Harald from his throne. "You must be joking! I've been happy to help you so far, but that's too much. You've got nothing but the clothes you're wearing. Ask me again when you're as rich as me, and famous too."

Harald turned and marched out of the palace, his face grim. Ulf and Haldor were waiting and Harald told them what the prince had said.

"The grumpy old so-and-so!" said Ulf. "What do we do now?"

"We could kidnap his daughter," said Haldor. "After dinner, that is."

"We wouldn't get very far," said Harald. "And I've got a better idea, anyway. He was wrong about me only having the clothes I'm wearing. I've got my sword as well, and I know where it will get me a fortune."

"You don't mean …" said Ulf and Haldor as if they had one voice.

"I do, lads," said Harald. "We're off to the Great City. We'll find ourselves the treasure we need in Constantinople."

Chapter 4

The Emperor's Bodyguard

Constantinople – 1034

Harald and his friends sailed south from Russia, down long rivers and into the Black Sea. They were heading for Constantinople, the biggest, richest city on earth at that time. It was called Constantinople because of the famous Roman Emperor Constantine, who had built it over 700 years before.

Now Constantinople was the capital of an empire. It was a city of towers and domes and palaces. More people lived there than anyone could count. The first Vikings who saw its enormous walls thought that giants must have built them. They called it 'Miklagard', which means 'The Great City' in Old Norse.

"What's the plan, Harald?" said Ulf when they sailed into the harbour. Haldor was far too busy staring at the city with his mouth open to talk.

"We're going to be the Emperor's bodyguards," said Harald. "I've heard that's where we'll make some money. Follow me, lads!"

Harald was right. Everyone knew the Vikings were the best fighters in the world – which is why the Emperor wanted them as his bodyguards. He paid them well and made sure they were well looked after, too. They had to fight in his wars, of course, but none of the Vikings minded that.

Harald led his friends to the Emperor's palace, and it didn't take him long to get what he wanted. The Emperor was impressed by this giant young Viking with his blond hair and cocky smile. And Ulf and Haldor were pretty impressed by the palace and all the Emperor's riches.

"Wow, I've never seen anything like it," said Haldor. "I bet the food is good here, too. Do you think we'll get something to eat soon?"

"Never mind that. Has Harald done the right thing?" muttered Ulf. "Who is that nasty-looking woman? Why is she staring at us like that?"

The woman was the Emperor's wife, the Empress Zoë. It turned out that she was the one who had the real power. The Emperor was her puppet, and he did what she told him.

Harald and his friends soon found out she was always plotting and making secret plans. No one at the palace was truly safe.

At first none of that bothered the young Vikings. They were too busy learning Greek, which is what everyone talked in Constantinople. They worked as the Emperor's bodyguards. And they went off to war as well. They fought in many strange and wonderful lands – Italy, Thrace, Palestine, Africa.

After a few years Harald was leader of the Emperor's bodyguard. He was famous all over the empire. He liked to make up poems about all he'd done, and he did get lots of treasure. He should have given it all to the Emperor. But he kept most of the loot and hid it away for himself.

"You'll get us all killed, Harald," Ulf muttered. "If Zoë finds out …"

"You worry too much," laughed Harald. "Everything will be fine!"

But it wasn't. Zoë did find out, and she was very very angry. She sent some of her own soldiers to catch Harald and they threw him in prison!

Chapter 5
Escape

Constantinople – 1043

Harald's prison was in a tower near the palace. There were plenty of guards. Harald was kept in chains and Zoë came to visit him every day. She loved seeing him chained up like a dog and she told him she was looking forward to having his head cut off and stuck on a pole. But like a true Viking, Harald just laughed at her.

Then one day Zoë didn't come. Harald could hear lots of noise outside in the city – the sound of shouting and screaming and fighting. Suddenly the door of his dungeon burst wide open – and Ulf and Haldor ran in.

"Nice to see you at last, lads," said Harald. "What took you so long?"

"We've been busy," said Ulf. "Besides, there wasn't much we could do, was there? If we'd tried to free you we'd have ended up in here too. Zoë has her spies everywhere – she'd have caught us if we'd done anything."

"But now's your chance!" said Haldor. "Her enemies are trying to get rid of her. There's fighting all over the city and the guards of your prison have fled."

"So that's what all that noise is about," said Harald. "What are you waiting for? I can't get these chains off by myself! Help me and we'll be rich again!"

Haldor smashed the chains with a few blows from his battle-axe, and Harald was free. The three friends ran out into the street, which was full of fighting and shouting.

Ulf wanted to make for the fort where the bodyguards lived, but Harald had other ideas.

"We don't know how things are going to turn out here," Harald said. Just then an arrow whizzed past over their heads. There was a group of Zoë's soldiers at the end of the street, and they were pointing and yelling at the young Vikings. "Zoë might win. I think it's time for us to go. There's something I've got to do in Russia. We need to get back there."

"That's all very well, Harald," muttered Ulf. More arrows flew past and the Vikings had to keep dodging and ducking them. "How are we going to get there? We don't have a ship."

"Oh yes we do," said Harald. "Come on, lads, I'll show you."

Harald made his friends run as fast as they could to the harbour and there was a ship ready and waiting for them. It was Harald's own ship and it was all set to sail back to Russia. Harald had his secret treasure all the time and he'd hidden it in the ship. The three friends jumped aboard. Soon they were heading out to sea, the arrows of the soldiers falling into the waves behind them.

****

When they got back to Russia, Harald, Ulf and Haldor marched into the palace of Prince Yaroslav and stood before him. To everyone there it looked as if the young Viking had grown even taller and bigger. He was stronger now, and he was tough. He looked rich as well, with thick gold necklaces and arm rings.

"I'm here to collect what you owe me, Yaroslav," said Harald, giving the prince a hard stare. "Am I rich and famous enough for you now?"

Prince Yaroslav was sitting on his throne. Elizabeth was standing beside him. She was smiling at Harald, and she gave her father a nudge.

"Oh, all right," the prince grumbled. "We'll arrange the wedding."

Harald grinned. But he was already thinking about the next thing he would do ...

Chapter 6
Half a Kingdom

Norway – 1044

The next thing Harald wanted to do was to go
home. He could have stayed in Russia, or gone
somewhere else to get some land for himself.
He was rich and famous enough now to do
almost anything he wanted. But his mind was
set on one thing alone – he wanted to be King of
Norway.

So not long after his wedding, Harald left Russia for ever. He took with him his new wife, his friends Ulf and Haldor, a small army – and 12 large chests full of treasure. He sailed across the Baltic Sea, marched through Sweden and at last he came to the border of Norway. There he stopped.

Things had changed in Norway. Harald's brother Olaf had left a son, whose name was Magnus. Magnus had fought the warlords who wanted to be kings of Norway all the time that Harald had been away. He'd beaten them all and now he was the King of Norway. He was King of Denmark too.

But Harald wanted to be King. Maybe not of all of Norway. Just some of the kingdom would be fine. He had a plan, a very simple one ...

"Why are we meeting your nephew here?" Ulf asked. "He doesn't have to talk to you. He might just ambush you and kill you instead."

"I don't care what he does. I'm too hungry to be bothered," said Haldor. "I'm starving!"

"Magnus will meet me all right," said Harald with a smile. "He'll want to talk to me because I've got something he wants."

"You can tell him all about it now," Ulf muttered. "He's arrived."

They looked round. Magnus was riding towards them. Behind him was an army much larger than Harald's. But Harald didn't seem worried.

"It's good to see you after so long, Magnus," he said. "How grown up you look! Why, when I left Norway you were still a baby."

Ulf and Haldor sniggered at that, and so did some of the men in Magnus's army. The young man turned to glare at them and they soon fell silent.

"Well, Uncle, I'm not a baby any more," said Magnus. "I'm a king."

"Ah, I wanted to talk to you about that," said Harald. "How would you like to give me part of your kingdom. Let's say ... half of it."

"Why would I want to do that?" said Magnus, laughing at him.

"Because you're broke," said Harald. He turned to his friends. "Show him the treasure, lads."

Ulf and Haldor flung the chests open, and the Greek gold glittered in the cold northern light. Magnus stared at it, and his eyes glittered too. Harald smiled. He'd heard from the traders in Kiev that Magnus had run out of money. So Harald had decided to use his treasure to buy some power, rather than fight for it. He knew Magnus had a bigger army than him.

'Half a kingdom is better than no kingdom at all,' Harald thought.

Besides, there was always the chance that he might get the other half another day.

Chapter 7
Funeral for a King

The Vikings liked to bargain with each other. It took Magnus and Harald a long time and a lot of haggling before they could agree. In the end, Magnus gave Harald half his kingdom in return for half the treasure. They sealed the deal with a handshake and some grand words, and then they settled down to rule together.

Things didn't go all that smoothly. It wasn't long before the two kings started arguing about everything – who should have the bigger throne, who should be served first at feasts, even who had the best-looking wife. Then something happened that solved the problem.

Magnus suddenly fell ill and died.

Ulf brought the news to Harald.

"I'm sorry to hear that," said Harald. "I didn't know he was sick."

"He wasn't," said Ulf. "At least not until after he had his dinner last night. People are saying that you put poison in his food."

"Yuck, what a terrible, disgusting thought," Haldor muttered.

"How can they think so badly of me?" said Harald with a sly grin. "But I suppose it does mean I can be king on my own."

Harald cried at his nephew's funeral. He even wrote a poem about what a wonderful king Magnus had been. They were family, after all.

But his tears soon dried, and the people of Norway and the countries near by soon found out what a hardnut he really was. That was when they started to call him Harald *Hardrada*. It was when Harald had his terrifying raven flag made. The years when he truly became a legend ...

The warlords of Norway knew who he was now. Harald found out who the men were that had plotted against his brother King Olaf – and then Harald had them killed. He kept the other nobles busy in his wars. He had one dangerous enemy left. After Magnus had died, a warlord called Sweyn had made himself King of Denmark. Sweyn and Harald hated each other.

Harald invaded Denmark every summer, and Sweyn invaded Norway back. Harald could have beaten Sweyn any time he liked. But they both enjoyed the fighting and looting and they

didn't want it to stop. The war between them lasted 15 years but in the end Harald won.

So the day came when Harald had no more enemies to fight. He was much older and now he spent his days running his kingdom, or hunting. He was still married to Elizabeth but, like most Viking rulers, he had a second wife. His new wife was called Thora but Harald still wasn't happy.

In fact, he was so grumpy that hardly anyone dared speak to him. By now Haldor was known as Fat Haldor, and he didn't speak much. Harald had made him rich and Haldor could eat as much as he liked and when he liked. His mouth was always full of food.

Ulf was the only person left to tell Harald what was what.

"All right, Ulf, don't keep on at me," Harald muttered one day. "I know I'm grumpy. I'm bored, that's all. I wish something exciting would happen for once."

A few weeks later Harald's wish came true.

Chapter 8
A Great Adventure

Norway – Spring 1066

One day a stranger rode up to Harald's great hall. The guards at the gate asked the man who he was, and what he wanted with the king. The stranger looked at them and smiled.

"Tell Harald that Tostig Godwinson has come a long way to see him," said the man. "And that I bring him the chance to win another kingdom."

Tostig was the brother of the new king of England. The new king of England had almost the same name as Harald. He was called Harold. Tostig had been Earl of Northumbria, but he'd made a real mess of things there. So Harold had sent Tostig away and made Morcar the new Earl. Tostig had left England to sulk. He was angry with his brother and he wanted revenge.

"Let me get this straight," said Harald when Tostig was standing in front of him. "You think that I could be King of England if I wanted?"

"Why not?" said Tostig. He was a tough-looking warrior himself. "I reckon you've got just as much right as Harold, and more than Duke William."

"What do you think, Ulf?" said Harald. He turned to his old friend.

"It depends," said Ulf. "There were some kings of Norway who were kings of England too.

You could be king of both Norway and England at the same time. But Harold isn't just going to hand you over his kingdom, is he? You'll have to take it from him."

Fat Haldor sat in the corner, silent and munching on a chicken leg.

"Ulf has a point, Tostig," said Harald. "It won't be easy, will it? I hear your brother is a good fighter, and that he has plenty of brave and skilful warriors."

"But who can stand against Harald Hardrada, the greatest Viking of all time?" said Tostig. "As soon as you land men will flock to your banner."

"Hang on a second," Ulf said crossly. "It all sounds too good to be true. What's in it for you, Tostig? Don't you want to be king yourself?"

"I'd just be happy to serve you, my lord," Tostig said in an oily voice, looking right at

Harald. "But of course I'd hope for some sort of reward ..."

"Yes, your brother's head on a pole, and maybe those of Morcar and Edwin as well," laughed Harald. "I'm sure that could all be arranged."

"You're not going to do this, are you, Harald?" said Ulf. "It's madness. You can't trust Tostig, and you're far too old. You're over fifty now ..."

"Oh, stop moaning, Ulf," said Harald with a scowl. "I'm fed up with listening to your doom and gloom. I'm off to England with Tostig. Why don't you come too? It'll be a great adventure. The storytellers will sing songs about it. I'll write a poem about it myself afterwards."

"If you're still alive," said Ulf. "No, you can count me out, Harald."

With that, Ulf turned and walked away.

Fat Haldor rose to his feet and stared at Harald for a moment. Then he belched ... and followed Ulf.

Harald never saw either of his friends again. Not in this life, anyway.

But at the time he didn't much care. He had a war to look forward to.

Chapter 9

A Surprise ... and Two Offers

England – September 1066

Harald set sail from Norway. The dragon heads of his fleet of 300 Viking longships pointed towards England. He landed his army on the coast of Yorkshire, then he moved inland to a place called Fulford Gate. And that's where Morcar and Edwin were waiting for him, on the road to York.

The battle with Morcar's men was over quickly. The Saxons were utterly defeated. Morcar and Edwin fled in panic with just a few of their warriors left alive.

"Not bad for an old man, eh, Tostig?" said Harald. He grinned and wiped the blood from his sword. "I haven't had that much fun in years."

"You were terrific," said Tostig. "Now I know why you're a legend."

"I'm a very warm legend at the moment," said Harald. It was a hot September day, and the sun was shining in the blue English sky. "I'll bet the men are feeling the heat too. We'd better let them rest for a while."

Harald told his men they could take off their chainmail and helmets and rest. Soon the army was sitting in a field near a river. They'd won their battle. Life looked good. Suddenly Harald heard a noise far off – the tramp,

tramp of marching feet, and the chink of iron weapons.

Harald stood up and watched an army march into the field on the other side of the river.

The sunlight glittered on their spear points and helmets, and a flag flew above them – the great white horse banner of Harold, King of England.

"I don't believe it," muttered Tostig. "That's my brother's army."

"Is it?" said Harald, unimpressed. "He got here pretty fast. I thought you said he'd be too worried about Duke William invading to march north."

"I ... I did," said Tostig. "But I was wrong."

Harald scowled at him. He told his men to prepare for battle. It was hard for them to put their chainmail back on quickly. A small group of riders from the English army crossed the river with a flag of truce. Harald put on his helmet and walked up to speak to them. Tostig went with him.

"I come with an offer for you, Tostig," said the grim-faced Saxon warrior at the head of the group. "You can be Earl of Northumbria again … but you must leave this Viking and swear loyalty to your king, Harold of England."

"No chance," laughed Tostig. "I think I'll stick with Harald Hardrada."

"Suit yourself," said the Saxon and turned to go.

"Hold on," said Harald. "Don't you have an offer for me?"

The Saxon stopped and looked at Harald. Then he smiled. "You're a big man, Harald Hardrada," he said. "But you can have a hole

in the English ground big enough to be your grave."

Then the Saxon rode away with his men.

"Charming!" said Harald. "Who was that, Tostig? Do you know him?"

"That was Harold, my brother," said Tostig. "I thought you knew it was him."

"I didn't. You should have told me," said Harald. "We could have dealt with him right here. Now we'll have to fight a battle instead."

Somehow he didn't look all that unhappy at the idea!

Chapter 10
The Last Battle

Things moved quickly after that, far too quickly for the Vikings to put on their chainmail or even their helmets. The Saxon army pushed across the river, and soon Harald's warriors were fighting for their lives. They did their best, but they were too easy to cut down. They'd just fought one battle and they were tired.

"To me, to me! Over here!" yelled Harald. His men gathered round him – this huge, laughing Viking with his blond hair and wild blue eyes. He fought like a demon from hell beneath his great raven banner. The sun glinted on his sword and made it seem as if he was using a lightning bolt for a weapon.

"Give in, Hardrada!" the English king shouted. "You've got no hope of winning. I'll spare all of you, even Tostig, if you surrender now."

"Very good of you," said Harald, stopping for breath. "But I'm not beaten yet. Still, I'm always open to a good offer. I tell you what – chuck in your kingdom and a dozen chests of gold, and we might have a deal."

The two mighty warriors smiled at each other across the battle. Then the English king sadly shook his head and ordered his men to attack once more. Harald strode forward to meet them. He swung his sword with both hands and hacked down every brave Saxon warrior who came before him.

But not even the greatest Viking of all time could win against such odds. At last a Saxon archer took careful aim ... and fired a deadly arrow that hit Harald's throat. He fell to the ground and a groan went up from the few Vikings who still lived.

One of them ran up to him and pulled out the arrow. Harald grunted.

"The man who fired that arrow knew what he was doing," he said. Then he smiled. "I only wish old Ulf was here to say I told you so. And I hope that idiot Tostig is dead by now."

"He is," said someone standing near by. Harald's eyes were growing dim and he couldn't see much, but he thought it must be Tostig's brother.

"Oh, well, it was fun while it lasted," said Harald, and in his mind he felt young again. He saw his friends Ulf and Haldor and his adventures in Russia and with the Emperor in

Constantinople. He saw his two wives and his treasure, and all his battles, and he smiled even more. Then with a sigh ... he died.

Harold had him wrapped in his raven banner, and a year later his body was taken back to Norway and buried.

A lot had happened in between.

Duke William did invade, and Harold had to hurry south to meet him. There was another great battle, this time near Hastings, and Harold's army was totally smashed. Harold himself was killed.

Duke William was crowned King of England, and from then on he was known as William the Conqueror, the first Norman king of England.

The age of the Vikings was over. But everyone agreed on one thing.

The name of Harald Hardnut would live for ever!

Our books are tested
for children and young people by
children and young people.

Thanks to everyone who consulted on
a manuscript for their time and effort in
helping us to make our books better
for our readers.